Jordan's Hair

JUDSON PRESS
PUBLISHERS SINCE 1824

Library of Congress Cataloging-in-Publication Data
Spruill, Ed.   Jordan's hair / Ed & Sonya Spruill; illustrated by Stephen Mercer Peringer.   p. cm.
Summary: A young African American boy discovers that being different from his friends at school is a good thing.
ISBN 978-0-8170-1484-1 (alk. paper) [1. Hair—Fiction. 2. Individuality—Fiction. 3. African Americans—Fiction. 4. Stories in
rhyme.] I. Spruill, Sonya. II. Peringer, Stephen Mercer, ill. III. Title. PZ8.3.S76945Jor 2005   [E]—dc22   2005012457

"Mom, other kids have good hair but I think my hair's bad.
And I don't like the way it looks. It even makes me mad.

My hair is hard and shorter; their hair is soft and long.
Tell me, when God made my hair, did God do
something wrong?"

"Jordan, your hair's perfect. Believe me, for it's true. I say it's perfect 'cause I know God gave your hair to you.

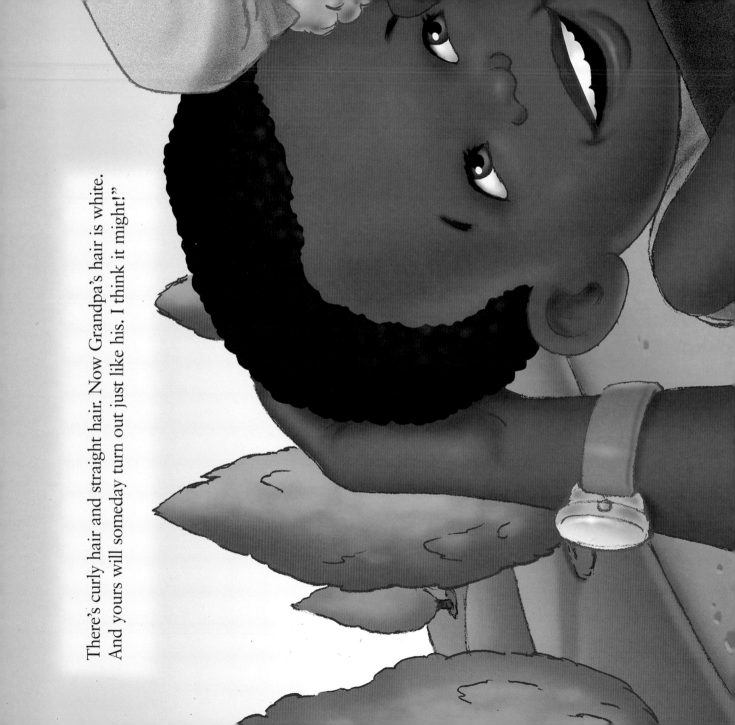

There's curly hair and straight hair. Now Grandpa's hair is white.
And yours will someday turn out just like his. I think it might!"

"Dad, why do I look different from everyone at school?
Why do I look like I do? To me, it seems so cruel.

My skin is brown but all my friends at school have skin that's white.
Will I look more like them if I can just sleep through the night?

I'm tired of being different. I don't want to look this way.
Will God make me look more like them tomorrow, if I pray?"

"Kids come in many colors, not only brown and white.

The color that God made them is the color that is right.

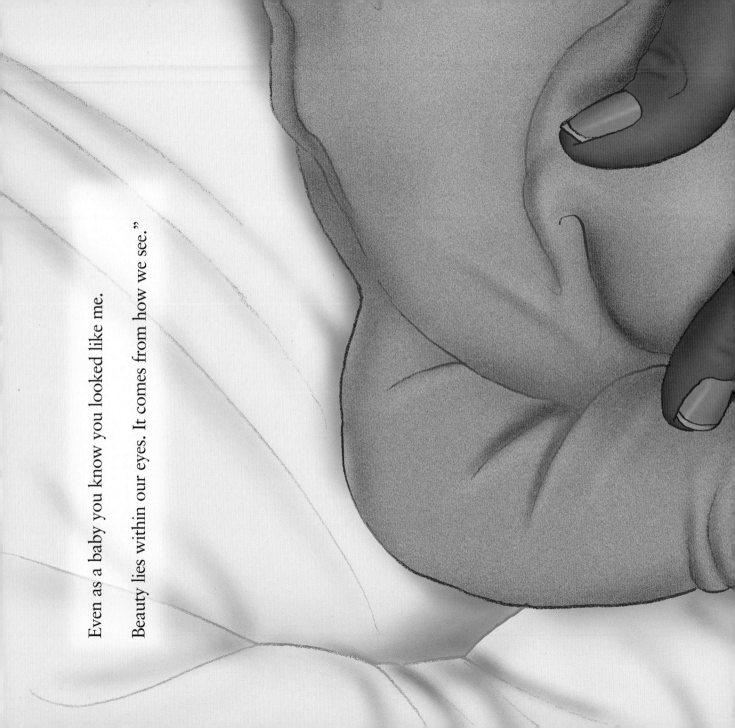

Even as a baby you know you looked like me.

Beauty lies within our eyes. It comes from how we see."

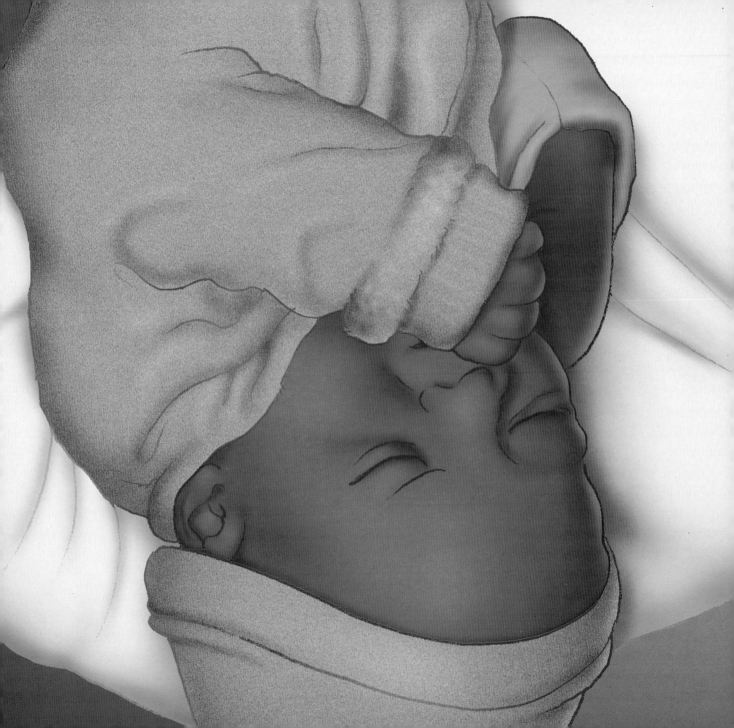

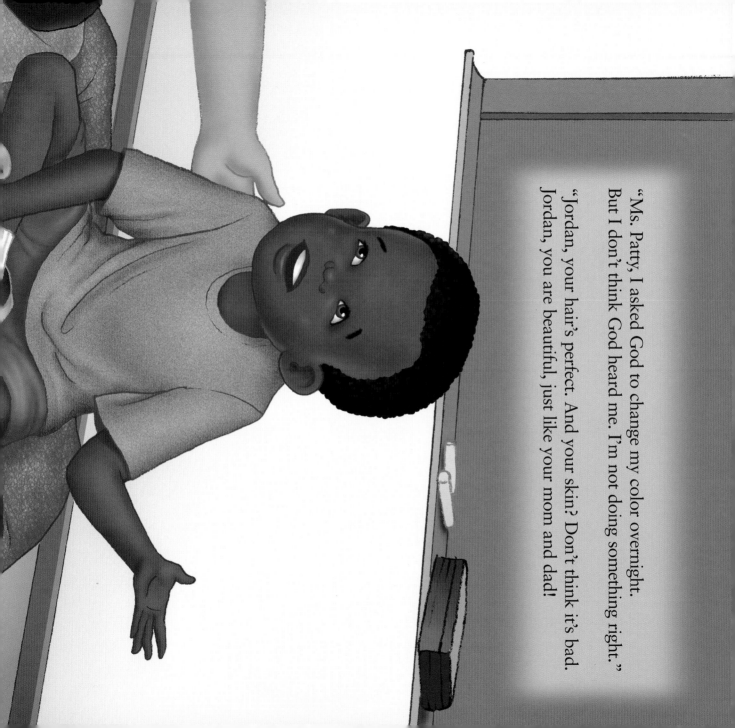

"Ms. Patty, I asked God to change my color overnight. But I don't think God heard me. I'm not doing something right."

"Jordan, your hair's perfect. And your skin? Don't think it's bad. Jordan, you are beautiful, just like your mom and dad!"

Now sometimes you might want to look like all your classmates do.
But did you know that sometimes your friends want to look like you?

It's not the way you look that makes them want to be your friend.
The outside doesn't matter, but what counts is deep within.

You laugh, you smile, you help your friends, you even share your toys.
And that's why you've become one of my very favorite boys!

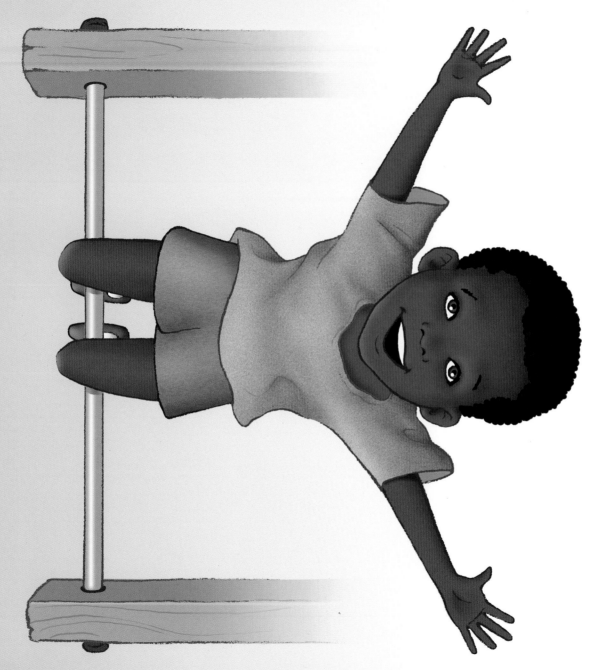

So don't let being different ever make you sad or blue.
Being different makes you special. Being different makes you you!"